I Love Hugs

by Lara Jones

Cartwheel
BOOKS®

SCHOLASTIC INC.

New York Toronto London Auckland Sydney
Mexico City New Delhi Hong Kong Buenos Aires

For Ness
with thanks

ISBN 0-439-64442-9

Text copyright © 2001 by Scholastic Ltd.
Illustrations copyright © 2001 by Lara Jones. All rights reserved.
Published by Scholastic Inc.
SCHOLASTIC, CARTWHEEL BOOKS, and associated logos are
trademarks and/or registered trademarks of Scholastic Inc.

12 11 10 9 8 7 6   8 9/0

Printed in the U.S.A.   23

First Scholastic paperback printing, February 2004

I love hugs.

This is my teddy.
He loves bear hugs.

My baby brother has
fallen down. He needs a
make-it-better hug.

Our cat has eaten
all of his dinner.
I'll give him a good-job hug.

This is Meg.
We share
best-friend
hugs.

Today is Sam's birthday.
My teddy gives him
a birthday hug.

It's getting late, so we have
time-to-go-home hugs.

At bedtime we have
good-night,
sleep-tight hugs.

I love hugs.